THE BIG BIRTHDAY SURPRISE
• JUNIOR DISCOVERS GIVING •

BY DAVE RAMSEY
ILLUSTRATED BY MARSHALL RAMSEY

COLLECT ALL SIX ADVENTURES AT DAVERAMSEY.COM!

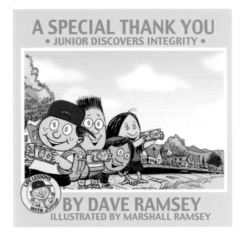

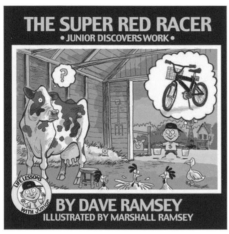

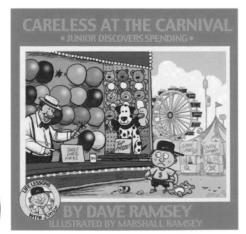

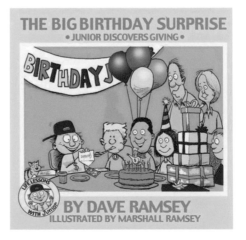

More fun than a barrel of money!

Dedication

Daniel is our youngest child and our only boy. He has learned a lot from his sisters.
They taught him quickly not to have a grocery store fit!

Thank you, Daniel, for having an open heart that is willing
to learn life principles from your family. And thank you
for having such a tender spirit . . . always thinking of others.

www.daveramsey.com

The children's group of Lampo Press

The Big Birthday Surprise: Junior Discovers Giving

Requests for information should be addressed to:
Lampo Press: 1749 Mallory Lane Suite #100 Brentwood, Tennessee 37027

ISBN 978-0-9726323-2-4

Second Edition

Written by: Dave Ramsey
Editors: Charlene Kever, Debbie LoCurto, Amber Kever and Darrin Dickey
Cover Design and Art Direction: Marshall Ramsey

Printed and bound in China.

For more information on Dave Ramsey, go to: www.daveramsey.com or call (888) 227-3223
For more information on Marshall Ramsey, go to: www.clarionledger.com/ramsey

Junior ran into the kitchen and looked at the calendar beside the refrigerator. "Only five more days until my BIRTHDAY PARTY!" Junior thought. "I wonder who will come?"

Junior's mom invited everyone... his friends from school and church and GRANDMOTHER! Grandmother promised an extra special gift for Junior this year. He could hardly wait to see it.

Junior imagined ALL the wonderful gifts he might get on his birthday. He wanted a drum set and a REAL guitar. He wanted a new ball glove, army men and a new video game. He could hardly wait to get presents!

Junior's mom called from the next room, "It's time for school." He grabbed his backpack and ran to catch the bus.

"Attention, Class," said Ms. Harper, Junior's teacher. "Principal Woodburn has assigned a BIG project to us. We'll be supplying food items for the downtown orphanage. Each student is asked to bring in three food items."

Travis raised his hand. "Why do they need food at the orphanage? Don't they have food?"

"Well, Travis," said Ms. Harper, "these children don't have moms and dads to care for them. The people who run the orphanage take care of them, and they depend on people in the community to give them food."

"Boys and girls, what does it mean to GIVE?" asked Ms. Harper.

Esther raised her hand and said, "It means that you offer something you have to help someone else in need."

"That's right, Esther," said Ms. Harper. "We're going to bring food from our homes to help the orphanage. Sharing with others who are in need will make you SMILE. Here is a list of the food items you can bring."

The bell rang as Ms. Harper was finishing, and Junior slipped the PROJECT 'GIVING' list into his backpack.

At dinner that night Junior asked, "May I please have one can of peas, one can of corn, two boxes of macaroni and cheese and one bag of chocolate chip cookies?"

"Oh my," said Mom, "are you that hungry?"

Junior began to laugh, "No, we have a BIG project at school and each student has been asked to bring food items for the orphanage downtown."

"That's a wonderful project," said Mom.

"I'm so glad you're GIVING to others," said Dad.

"I'm glad we have plenty of food since the orphans need some," said Junior. "Just like Dollar Bill always says, 'Giving makes you less selfish!'"

"Well, Dollar Bill is exactly right," said Dad. "It's just like each week when we go to church, we give to the church in order to help others."

Junior smiled, "Thanks, Mom, for letting us share our food with the orphans."

Mom gave Junior a big hug and said, "I'm so proud of you for sharing with others."

...dnesday morning all of the students brought ...ood items for PROJECT 'GIVING'. There were boxes and cans of food all over the room!

"Children, this is wonderful! The children at the orphanage will have so much food! You have done a great job!" exclaimed Ms. Harper.

"I have chosen two students from the class to help deliver the food to the orphanage. Michelle and Junior, you'll come with me to deliver the food."

Junior was so excited! He and Michelle loaded all the food from the classroom into the school van. Then Michelle and Junior hopped into the van and Ms. Harper drove them to the orphanage.

Junior walked inside the orphanage and was greeted by all the boys and girls. They were so excited to have visitors! They hugged Ms. Harper and hugged Michelle and even hugged Junior and yelled, "THANK YOU FOR THE FOOD!"

Junior was able to play with some of the children while Ms. Harper talked to the adults at the orphanage. He noticed a boy sitting out on the porch all by himself. Junior walked over to him and said, "Hi, my name is Junior. What's your name?"

"Hi, Junior. My name is Chris Thomas." Junior and Chris began to play in the yard. They played tag and climbed a tree.

"Hey, Chris, want to play catch with me?" asked Junior.

"We don't have a baseball," said Chris. "We don't have many things to play with here at the orphanage."

"Really?" said Junior. "I can't imagine not having a baseball and glove."

"It's okay, we just make up our own fun!" said Chris.

Junior heard Ms. Harper coming through the door with Michelle. "There you are, Junior," said Ms. Harper. "We need to go back to school now. Say goodbye to your friend."

Junior said goodbye to Chris and gave him a HIGH FIVE!

"I've had fun playing," said Junior.

"Me, too," said Chris, "see you later."

Ms. Harper, Junior and Michelle loaded into the van and drove back to school.

"It looks like you made a friend, Junior," said Ms. Harper.

"Yes, I did," said Junior. "His name is Chris and he's super nice. We played tag and climbed a tree, but he didn't have a ball or glove so we couldn't play catch."

"Why didn't he have a ball and glove?" asked Michelle.

"He said they don't have many toys at the orphanage, but he wasn't sad. Chris said they can make up their own fun!" answered Junior.

Later that night Junior's parents came to tuck him into bed. "How was your day, Junior?" asked Mom.

"It was GREAT!" replied Junior. "I helped Ms. Harper deliver ALL our food items to the orphanage."

"What was it like?" asked Mom.

"I made a new friend. His name is Chris. We climbed a tree and played tag, but we couldn't play catch because he didn't have a ball or glove," said Junior.

"Junior, I'm proud of you giving not only the food items, but giving your time at the orphanage today," said Dad.

"Me, too," said Junior. "It was great fun!"

"It's time to go to sleep now. We have a full couple of days ahead and then, do you know what happens in three days?" asked Mom.

"It's my BIRTHDAY PARTY!" exclaimed Junior.

"Yes," said Mom, "It's your BIRTHDAY PARTY. And remember GRANDMOTHER is bringing you a very special gift this year! Good night Junior, say your prayers." Junior's mom kissed him on his forehead and turned out the lights.

Junior woke up very early Saturday morning. He ran downstairs to look at the calendar one more time. "Today is my BIRTHDAY!" yelled Junior.

"Yes, TODAY is your BIRTHDAY, Junior. HAPPY BIRTHDAY!" said Mom, as she gave him a big hug. "We have lots to do before all your birthday guests arrive! We need to bake your cake and decorate for your party and, Junior, you have to clean your room!"

"Yes, ma'am," said Junior and he ran upstairs to clean his room.

A few hours later the doorbell started ringing. ALL of Junior's friends were there . . . Billy Hampton, Esther, Travis, Michelle, Charlene, and Joe; they just kept coming through the door. And EVERYONE brought a BIRTHDAY gift for Junior. He got so many presents that his mom had to stack them up high on the table.

Finally, GRANDMOTHER arrived. Junior gave her a super big hug. He looked for his extra special BIRTHDAY SURPRISE, but GRANDMOTHER didn't have a big gift, only a small envelope with Junior's name on it.

Junior's mom called everyone into the kitchen. It was time for the birthday cake! Junior stood in front of the big birthday cake, which was glowing from all of the candles, and everyone started to sing, "HAPPY BIRTHDAY TO YOU, HAPPY BIRTHDAY TO YOU, HAPPY BIRTHDAY DEAR JUNIOR, HAPPY BIRTHDAY TO YOU."

When they finished singing, GRANDMOTHER said, "It's time to blow out the candles, Junior." Junior leaned way back, taking in a huge breath of air…leaned forward…and blew ALL the candles out with one big breath. Everyone cheered!

"Okay, you can start opening your presents now," said Junior's mom.

Junior grabbed the first gift and tore the paper off…it was a video game he wanted. Then he opened a set of official army men and a new ball and glove. Junior got so many gifts. He even got a drum set and guitar from his parents!

The only gift left to open was the envelope from GRANDMOTHER.

"Junior, it's time to open my very special gift to you," said GRANDMOTHER.

He picked up the envelope and began tearing it at one end. He couldn't believe it as he pulled out a crisp, new one hundred dollar bill!

"WOW!" exclaimed Junior. "I've never had a one hundred dollar bill. Can I buy anything I want?"

"Yes, Junior," said GRANDMOTHER. "The one hundred dollar bill is yours to do whatever YOU want."

Junior hugged his GRANDMOTHER tight and thanked her for the BIG BIRTHDAY SURPRISE! He thanked all his friends for the wonderful gifts and then he and his friends ran to the backyard to play with all of his new toys.

Junior had so much fun with his friends and all his new toys. He already started thinking about all the things he could buy with his one hundred dollar bill . . . he could buy tickets to a movie or another video game . . . he could get a pair of roller blades . . . maybe he could buy it ALL with his one hundred dollar bill.

But as Junior was playing catch with Billy, he thought of his new friend at the orphanage, Chris. "Chris doesn't even have a ball and glove," thought Junior, "and I got ALL these gifts today!"

Later that afternoon when all his friends were gone, Junior thought again about Chris and the other boys and girls at the orphanage. He looked in his closet and under his bed and saw all the toys he hardly ever played with anymore.

Then Junior had an idea. He ran into the living room and asked his mom and dad, "Can I take all my toys that I don't play with anymore to the orphanage? And on the way, could we please stop at the sports store?"

"Junior, I think that's a great idea! Go gather up all the toys you want to take, and we'll go right now," said Dad.

When they arrived at the orphanage, Junior grabbed a huge box of toys out of the car and ran to ring the doorbell.

"Well, hello, Junior. What's all this?" asked the lady at the orphanage.

"It's toys for all the boys and girls here!" Junior had a little bit of everything in the box . . . building blocks and stuffed animals, a football and basketball, a robot and a remote controlled car. The children were so happy!

Junior walked around the orphanage to find Chris and saw him playing outside. He ran out and handed him a big package from the sports store.

"What's this?" asked Chris.

"It's for you. It's MY BIG BIRTHDAY SURPRISE," said Junior. "The best thing I could think of to do with my GRANDMOTHER'S special gift is share it with you!" Chris opened the package and inside was a new baseball bat, ball and glove! "WOW!" exclaimed Chris. "Thank you so much, Junior!"

Junior and Chris played catch for a while. Then, as Junior and his dad drove home, Junior was smiling from ear to ear. "Junior," said Dad, "You were a GREAT giver today! I am very proud of you."

"Thanks, Dad. It was fun to see Chris so excited," said Junior. "Giving makes you think less of yourself and more of others! Giving really does make you less selfish. GRANDMOTHER'S gift was such a BIG BIRTHDAY SURPRISE!"